World's Scariest "True" Ghost Stories

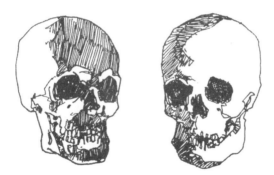

Margaret Rau

Illustrated by Jim Sharpe

Sterling Publishing Co., Inc.
New York

Library of Congress Cataloging-in-Publication Data

Rau, Margaret.
  World's scariest "true" ghost stories / Margaret Rau ; illustrated by Jim
Sharpe
      p.   cm.
  Includes index
  ISBN 0-8069-0796-7
  1. Ghosts—Juvenile literature. 2. Haunted houses—Juvenile literature. 3.
Ghost stories—Juvenile literature. [1. Ghosts. 2. Haunted houses.] I. Sharpe,
Jim, ill. II. Title.
 BF1461.R38 1994
 133.1—dc2094   94–16579
                                                                 CIP
                                                                  AC

10 9 8 7 6 5 4 3 2 1

Published by Sterling Publishing Company, Inc.
387 Park Avenue South, New York, N.Y. 10016
© 1994 by Margaret Rau
Illustrations © 1994 by Jim Sharpe
Distributed in Canada by Sterling Publishing
℅ Canadian Manda Group, P.O.Box 920, Station U
Toronto, Ontario, Canada M8Z 5P9
Distributed in Great Britain and Europe by Cassell PLC
Villiers House, 41/47 Strand, London WC2N 5JE, England
Distributed in Australia by Capricorn Link (Australia) Pty Ltd.
P.O. Box 6651, Baulkham Hills, Business Centre, NSW 2153, Australia
Manufactured in the United States of America
All rights reserved

Sterling ISBN 0-8069-0796-7

CONTENTS

1. MURDER WILL OUT

- A child loves to spend time in the attic—with a playmate no one else has ever seen . . .

- A hanged man's curse proves his innocence . . .

- Two grinning skeletons reveal a long-forgotten double murder . . .

- A phantom points to the place where his body lies . . .

The Boy with the Brass Buttons

The old-fashioned house in Stuyvesant Square caught the eye of a young couple who had just arrived in Philadelphia that winter day in 1889. They bought it and moved in with their little six-year-old daughter.

There was a lot of refurbishing to be done, so it was nice to have an attic in which the little girl could play while the rest of the house was being worked on. The previous owners, the Cowderys, had turned the attic into a playroom. It even had a fireplace, though it was now boarded up.

After a couple of weeks, the downstairs rooms were finished. The mother, realizing she hadn't seen much of her daughter in the past fortnight, planned to spend more time with her. But the little girl wasn't interested. She kept stealing away to the attic.

"What's so interesting up there in that stuffy room?" the exasperated mother asked at last.

"It's the little boy with the shiny buttons," the child replied. "He's so much fun to play with."

"What little boy?" her mother demanded, wondering if a servant's child had somehow stowed away in the room. She went to investigate. But the room was empty.

Certain that her daughter was just being stubborn, the mother appealed to her husband to discipline the child. At her father's stern voice, the little girl became hysterical. She kept repeating that there was a little boy and that he wore a blue jacket with lots of shiny buttons on it.

As her father listened, he became more and more curious. Formerly a seaman, he recognized her description of the buttons. They were probably brass and part of a child's sailor suit. He made some inquiries about the Cowderys, the family who had lived in the house before him. He learned that they had come from England with their children, two boys and a girl. The youngest child, a boy, was retarded. The neighbors described him as an idiot child.

According to the boy's parents, they went on, the young boy had always loved the nearby river. One day he had sneaked away on his own to play on its banks. He had fallen into the water and drowned. His body was never recovered, but his cap had been found floating on the river. Shortly after the child's disappearance, the Cowderys put the house up for sale and, leaving Philadelphia, dropped out of sight.

The former seaman's suspicions were now thoroughly aroused. He accompanied his little daughter to the attic and asked her to show him where the boy came from. She pointed to the boarded-up fireplace. Her father called in workers to open it and then to remove the mortar that cemented up a cavity in the wall beside the chimney.

As the mortar was chipped away, the corpse of a small boy was revealed. He was clothed in a little blue sailor jacket with four rows of brass buttons down the front. Examination showed that the back of the child's skull had been crushed.

No accidental drowning! Cold-blooded murder!

The Cursed Weed Patch

In 1821, John Newton of Newtown, Montgomeryshire, Wales, was brought to trial for murder. He vehemently proclaimed his innocence. But his protestations were ignored. He was convicted on purely circumstantial evidence and the testimony of two Welshmen who, Newton claimed, would profit from his death.

It was all to no avail. He was convicted and the judge sentenced him to death by hanging. Staring at the judge, his eyes burning, Newton shouted, "I am innocent! And to prove my innocence I will allow no grass to grow on my grave forever!"

John Newton was hanged in a public ceremony that, strangely enough, took place in a sudden fierce thunderstorm that filled the onlookers with misgivings. After the hanging, his corpse was buried in the country churchyard. The grave was unmarked by any headstone. All the same, it was easy to pick out. Among all the green graves in the cemetery, it alone was covered with sprawling weeds that followed the oblong pattern of the coffin lying below.

The unseemly grave appeared to be proclaiming the

innocence of the dead man. To blot out a growing sense of guilt in the little town, officials realized that if grass was going to grow on the grave, they'd have to make it happen themselves. Rich soil was brought in and spread over the grave. Grass seeds were planted. The soil was then watered and tended carefully. But none of the seeds sprouted. The patch of unsightly weeds remained.

By 1852 the Reverend Robert Mostyn Price took up the cause of the hanged man.

"Thirty years have passed," he wrote, "and we cannot grow any grass on this grave. I and others believe that this is proof that the poor man was innocent."

But it's difficult for human beings to accept the fact that justice has miscarried and caused the death of an innocent man. Once again an effort was made to grow grass on Newton's grave. Fresh rich soil was spread. The finest and hardiest grass seeds known were sown there, and the little plot was again carefully watered and tended.

A few grass shoots sprang up, but they were quickly smothered by a fresh crop of straggly weeds. The ugly little patch continued to stand out starkly in the lush green expanse of the graveyard.

Even over a century later, in 1941, a visitor to the cemetery was able to pick out the spot at once. The coffin-sized patch of weeds was still there among the green, neatly manicured graves of its sleeping companions, giving mute testimony to justice gone awry and a Welshman's curse!

Ghost with the Bloodstained Hands

I'll call them Jan and Mark Jackson, because they don't want any publicity about their weird experience. It was 1965 when it took place. The couple was living in an apartment on the third floor of an old Colonial-style house on Decatur Street in the French Quarter of New Orleans. Jan and Mark loved their apartment, with its charming, old-fashioned air. They didn't even mind most of the strange things that kept happening.

For instance, the clock on the living room mantel kept stopping every night at 3 A.M. and had to be reset every morning. And sometimes the Jacksons glimpsed a couple of shadowy figures that vanished as quickly as they appeared.

But there was one ghost that made them shiver. It was the ghost of a young woman in a filmy white gown that kept drifting through the rooms, her pleading eyes wide with shock and horror, her bloodstained hands clasped against her breast. This ghost upset the Jacksons so much that they began to ask questions about the old house. The answers led them to a story about something that had happened in the apartment back in 1910. At that time a young married woman was renting the Jacksons' apartment, where she was secretly meeting her lover. One day both she and her lover disappeared. It was suspected that the woman's jealous husband had found out about the affair and murdered them. But since the bodies were never found, there could also be another simpler explanation—one that the husband suggested—that the two had simply run away together. So, after the first flurry of headlines, the newspapers had dropped the subject and the story was forgotten.

Because of the ghost with the bloodstained hands, the Jacksons were convinced it was a case of murder and that the bodies had been hidden somewhere nearby. But where? Mark got his answer the day he went up to the attic to get something he had stored away.

In a corner, he noticed several rotted floorboards. Planning to replace them, he pulled them out and found himself looking down at two skeletons in the space below. Lying side by side, they were grinning up at him with gaping jaws. On the rib cage of one lay the blood-encrusted knife that must have killed them.

The Jacksons talked it over and decided that since both murderer and murdered were long dead, there would be no purpose in announcing their find. That night, they secretly buried the skeletons in a single grave. From that time on, the ghost with the blood-stained hands walked no more. And the clock on the mantel—that had obviously been marking the hour of the murder—continued ticking the night through.

The Most Honored Ghost

The most famous phantom in all Australia is the ghost of Frederick George James Fisher of Campbelltown, New South Wales, who was murdered in 1826. Fisher was a convict sent to Australia for a minor offense. He made good in his new country as the first man to manufacture paper in New South Wales. And he accumulated enough capital to purchase a 30-acre farm watered by a stream that flowed through his property.

The land next to Fisher's was rented by George

Worrall, another convict settler. The two men became close friends. For a time Fisher even lived at Worrall's home.

Then, on June 17, 1826, Fisher suddenly disappeared. Worrall explained that his friend had run away to England to escape a charge of forgery that was being brought against him. Meanwhile, Worrall claimed that, in his absence, Fisher had made him overseer of his estate.

As time went on, Worrall began taking more and more liberties with Fisher's possessions. People began whispering about murder, especially when Worrall tried selling a horse that had belonged to Fisher. The whispers grew louder when he tried to sell some timber he had taken from a grove of trees on Fisher's property. Finally, Worrall offered to pay $80 for the title deed to Fisher's land, which was being held against a debt Fisher owed a man named Daniel Cooper.

But suspicions are only suspicions and there was still no real proof that Fisher had not fled to England as Worrall claimed.

Then one day a special constable named Farley was walking along the fence that separated Fisher's farm from Worrall's. He was startled to see a man either climbing or leaning against the fence in the southeastern corner of the Fisher property. The man's face was turned towards the creek, but Farley recognized the figure as Fisher. As Farley watched, Fisher raised his arm, pointing his forefinger in the direction of the creek.

Astonished at the man's sudden return, Farley called out Fisher's name. At this, the figure vanished.

Farley hurried to the section of the fence where he had seen the ghost. Examining the rails, he saw massive blood stains.

With this new information, a concentrated search was made for Fisher's corpse. On October 20, 1826, two state troopers uncovered it in a swampy section of the creek bank, exactly where the ghost had pointed. Worrall was taken into custody, tried, convicted and hanged in February, 1827.

As for Farley, any suspicion that he might have made up the story to urge on the investigation was dispelled as he lay dying in 1841. When asked by reporters if he had concocted the story, he replied, "I'm a dying man. I'll speak only the truth. I saw that ghost as plainly as I see you now."

Fisher's body was buried in the graveyard of St. Peter's Church in Campbelltown. The grave was unmarked, and today its exact location is unknown. But Fisher's ghost is not forgotten. A festival to celebrate its appearance was first held in Campbelltown in 1856. Since then, the week-long festival in honor of the ghost has been held every year or two. A Fisher's Ghost Ball and other entertainments do honor to the age-old phantom. He is probably the only ghost in the world who is honored with a festival.

2. MYSTIFYING!

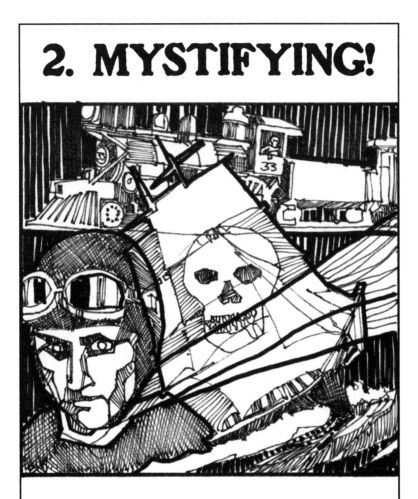

- Disabling burns appear from nowhere . . .

- A dead man drives engine No. 33 . . .

- A phantom aviator crashes his ghost plane . . . again and again . . .

- A jinxed ship is taken over by ghosts . . .

Burned Up

Dr. E. J. Sullivan always thought the statement "It burned me up" was only a metaphor. In his case it turned out to be much more.

It was April 24, 1970. Dr. Sullivan, a retired U.S. Naval Commander, had just lost his beloved wife of many years and had spent the day making the final funeral arrangements. Overcome with grief and a kind of hopeless fury at his loss, he flung himself on the bed in his hotel room and gave himself up to a despair so deep that he blanked out.

He lay there, lost in a trancelike state, until he was roused by the ringing of his telephone. He tried to get up to answer it, but found he couldn't move. He could not even open his hands, which were clenched into fists. He looked at them in shock. They were covered with huge blisters that spread up his arms. His feet and legs were also covered with blisters. Instead of feeling pain, his hands, arms, feet and legs had lost all sensation of any kind.

Unable to move, he could only cry out for help. At last, a hotel worker heard him and broke into the room. Sullivan asked to have his personal physician, Dr. George M. Lawton, called in. Dr. Lawton diagnosed the blisters as having been caused by electrical burns, though he couldn't understand how that could have happened. Sullivan had not been near any kind of electrical outlet, and the covers of the bed on which he lay had not even been scorched. The burns were so serious, however, that Dr. Lawton ordered his patient to a hospital.

As they waited for the ambulance to arrive, Sullivan noticed the time on his watch. It was six o'clock the evening of April 25. Twenty-four hours had gone by since he had flung himself on the bed in his hotel room.

The burns on Dr. Sullivan's hands turned out to be so deep that they destroyed his ability to grip things. This damage appeared to be permanent, despite many hours of physical therapy. Dr. Sullivan was at a loss to explain the mystery. At last, he could account for it only by one extraordinary answer. His fury and despair at losing his wife had literally burned him up with an emotion so fiery, it had emblazoned the deep electrical burns on his body.

The Runaway Locomotive

In January of 1892 engineer J. M. Pinkney visited his friend, a seasoned engineer on the old Northern Pacific Eastbound Overland train. Pinkney's friend covered a stretch of track that crosses the Cascade Mountains of the northwest United States.

As the friends sat together in the engineer's cab of the locomotive, they regaled each other with harrowing accounts of accidents that had occurred on their lines. Pinkney enjoyed most of the stories, but he couldn't take them seriously when they featured the paranormal. As hardheaded a man as you could find, he certainly didn't believe in ghosts.

As the train neared Eagle Gorge, the most dangerous spot on the 2,500–mile run, the engineer embarked on the story of old Tom Cypher. Cypher, he said, was an engineer who had died in an accident here two years before.

Suddenly, the engineer grasped the throttle and threw it over, reversing the engine. Then he applied the air brakes, bringing the train to a standstill. The spot where he had stopped was just a few feet short of the place where Cypher had met his death.

Pinkney couldn't understand why the engineer had stopped the train. There had been no hint of any danger. The night was clear and the track was empty. The engineer explained vaguely that some of the machinery had shaken loose and had to be tightened. In a few minutes, he said, they would be on their way.

As they started forward once more, Pinkney pointed out that there had been nothing wrong with the machinery, so why the stop?

"Look there!" his friend told him. "Don't you see it?"

Staring out of the cab window, Pinkney saw the headlights of a locomotive just 300 yards ahead. Shocked, he automatically reached for the lever to stop the train. His friend pushed his hand away, laughing.

"It's only old Tom Cypher's engine, No. 33," he said. "We won't collide. Because that man at the throttle is Cypher himself and, dead though he may be, he can go faster backwards than any man alive can go forwards. I've seen it 20 times before. Every engineer on this road looks for it."

Pinkney felt the hairs on his neck stand up as he watched the engine ahead of them, its headlights throwing out rays of red, green and white light. It had begun running silently backwards, remaining only a short distance ahead of them. Pinkney glimpsed a shadowy figure at the throttle. Then the locomotive rounded a curve and disappeared from view.

The train on which Pinkney was riding now began passing several small stations. At each one, the station master, fearful of an impending collision, warned the engineer to watch out for a runaway engine, No. 33, that was travelling backwards just a short distance ahead of them.

The engineer only laughed. "It's just old Cypher playing a prank," he said.

Pinkney still couldn't believe that a ghost had been at the throttle of that locomotive. Worried, he sent a telegram to the next station, which was in the town of Sprague, asking if No. 33 with a daredevil engineer aboard had been stopped.

The strange reply came back. "Rogue locomotive No. 33 has just arrived, her coal exhausted, her boxes burned out. No engineer at the throttle."

The Phantom Biplane

On May 27, 1963, Sir Peter Masefield, well known in aviation lore, was flying a DeHavilland Chipmunk from Dalcross to Shoreham, England. Masefield was going by way of the abandoned RAF airfield at Montrose. As he approached the airfield, he suddenly saw before him an ancient biplane, a plane with two pairs of supporting wings placed one above the other. It was the type of plane the RAF used for training before World War I.

The plane was close enough so that Masefield could see the aviator, who was dressed in a leather helmet, goggles and the silken scarf that was part of every old-time aviator's wardrobe. As Masefield stared, the biplane's upper right wing broke loose from its struts. The craft spun crazily in midair and then spiralled to the ground and crashed.

In horror, Masefield landed at a nearby golf course among a group of startled players. He shouted to them for help. Though the golfers had heard and seen nothing of a crash, they followed Sir Peter to the abandoned airfield. It was empty.

The experience was so disturbing to Masefield that he made inquiries at the Accidents Investigation Committee headquarters of the RAF. He found two entries dated June 2 and June 10, 1913. They described an accident that had taken place on the 27th of May, 1913. A training plane flown by Lieutenant Desmond Arthur had lost its upper right wing and crashed at Montrose field on that date.

Young Lieutenant Arthur was Irish, from County Clare. When he died, he was given a burial with full military honors. But in 1916 an official report attributed the loss of his plane to negligence and his memory was blackened.

From that time on, the ghost of Lieutenant Arthur was seen at No. 2 Mess Hall, where he had lived. It was always dressed in the full uniform of an aviator. It appeared so often that it became known as the "Irish Apparition."

Soon the ghost began to show up in other parts of the base. When guards challenged the ghost, it would disappear before their eyes, sending them fleeing in terror.

The story of the ghost spread through the RAF and beyond. It began appearing in newspapers across

England, where it came to the attention of an editor for a British flying magazine. He concluded that the dead aviator wanted his name cleared and insisted that the RAF make a further investigation into the cause of the crash. This time the RAF found that the blame lay not on the aviator but on the poor maintenance of the aircraft. The honor of the dead aviator restored, the Irish Apparition made its last appearance on earth in January of 1917.

But the daredevil young pilot must have still been haunting the airwaves above Montrose, when on May 27, 1963—the fiftieth anniversary of his death—he repeated his spectacular crash for the benefit of Sir Peter Masefield, one of Great Britain's most renowned aviators.

Jinxed Ship

One day in 1869 a workman was inspecting a fishing schooner, the *Charles Haskell*, for possible damage. He slipped on the steps of the companionway leading to the hold, fell and broke his neck, dying instantly. A single mishap like this usually is chalked up to carelessness or coincidence. But this happened in Newfoundland, Canada, where fishermen who face the dangers of northern waters are likely to take every accident aboard ship as a sign that it is jinxed or cursed.

Certainly, the captain and crew of the *Haskell* believed this. They deserted the ship immediately.

The owner, unable to find anyone willing to sign on, sold the schooner to a Captain Curtis of Gloucester, Massachusetts. The captain was a no-nonsense man who didn't believe in curses. He had some difficulty finding men to work for him at first, but the pay he offered was good and soon he had a crew. The *Charles Haskell* was back fishing again on the Grand Banks, a series of shoals off Newfoundland.

Everything went well until 1870, when a hurricane struck the Grand Banks. The hundred or so fishing ships gathered there were tossed about like matchsticks. One huge comber lifted the *Charles Haskell* and hurled it like a battering ram against the *Andrew Johnson*, which was smashed to pieces, killing everyone aboard. Though badly crippled, the *Haskell* managed to limp back to port.

Most fishermen would have considered that part of the *Haskell*'s curse. But since it was the *Andrew Johnson* that went down, the crew felt it didn't apply to them. Once the ship was repaired, it was back on the Grand Banks again.

For six days the crew of the *Charles Haskell* fished without incident. But on midnight of the seventh day, the watchmen standing guard spied movement in the waters around the ship. As they watched, 26 figures wearing rain slickers began rising out of the sea. One by one, they boarded the schooner. Staring straight ahead through eyeless sockets, they took up stations along the ship's railing. There they went through the motions of fishing.

Frozen with terror, the guards were unable to move until the phantoms put away their imaginary nets and fishing rods and returned back to the sea. Then they rushed to the captain's cabin, gabbling out an account of what they had seen.

Captain Curtis couldn't understand a word they were saying. But he saw stark fear in their eyes and ordered the ship back to port at once. It was well on its way by dawn. In the bright light of day the night's terrors seemed foolish. The captain was on the verge of returning to the Grand Banks when one of the crew shouted, "Look!"

Gaping, captain and crew watched as the 26 figures in rain slickers again rose from the sea and boarded the schooner. Once more they took up fishing positions along the rail. Finding his voice at last, the captain ordered full sail for port. But fast as the ship went, it could not shake the phantom fishermen. They stayed aboard until the port finally came into view. Then they climbed over the side of the ship. But this time, instead of sinking into the sea, they started walking across the sparkling waters towards the port, where they disappeared.

Who were they? Demons from the deep? The drowned men of the *Andrew Johnson*? No one took the time to ask. As soon as they docked, captain and crew fled, never to return.

No others came to take their place. The *Charles Haskell* was left to rot away in its berth. It never sailed again.

3. WHERE EVIL LURKS

- Terrifying forces haunt Nagoon Park . . .

- A beautiful phantom reveals her ancient crime . . .

- Old Man Ferreby wanted his house to stay in the family—even if he had to make it happen from beyond the grave . . .

- Does the ghost of a madman still haunt Discovery Gallery?

The Power at Nagoon Park

In the daytime Nagoon Park seems a pleasant enough place, lying about four miles away from the town of Manistee on the western side of Lake Michigan. It's woodsy with meadowlands, the home of birds and squirrels, bright and busy. But at dusk a different atmosphere settles over the silent haunted acres. Then it becomes dark and foreboding. There are accounts of lights flickering, jumbles of voices and the screams of a woman and children, riding on sudden gusts of wind that seem to rise from nowhere.

Brian Williams, a newcomer to town, had heard all kinds of stories about the park. Some said it was once the sacred haunt of ancient Indian shamans, who practiced their secret rituals in it. Others spoke of a witches' cult performing strange ceremonies there after dark. And then there was the horrible account of a farmer who once lived there with his wife and a brood of children. One night, in a mad rage, the farmer murdered the whole family, swinging right and left with a bloody axe.

Whatever the reason, all agreed on the dark nature of the park. So bad was its reputation that the city ordered it closed at dusk, the only park in the whole area that was shut down after sunset.

When Brian first heard all these stories, he was amused by them. Well educated and with a college degree, he was not given to what he considered superstition. One day he decided to put a period to all the town lore with a little commonsense action. He'd drive out to Nagoon Park at dusk and prove there was nothing in the tales. Though the park was closed, he'd get as close to it as possible and spend the night.

It wasn't hard to find other recruits—his girlfriend and another skeptical young couple. They decided to make a lark of it. At dusk they piled into Brian's car and drove down the country road in high spirits, stopping as close to the park entrance as they could.

Outside the car all was silent and motionless. The dark shapes of trees in the park hovered high against the sky like a wall, vague, menacing. The air had an uncanny stillness. The heavy silence seemed to flow out of the park like a thick tide. The voices of the young people sounded loud in the night. There was a shrill, almost hysterical cackle to their laughter.

Then, in the stillness, something outrageous happened. The rear of the car started to rise. The couples fell silent, staring at one another. Was it their imagination? Surely it couldn't really be happening.

Higher and higher rose the back of the car. Brian found himself sliding against the steering wheel, staring down at the hood, which was slanting noticeably downwards. And still the rear of the car kept rising until it was some four or five feet above the ground and almost perpendicular to the road. It would have taken a crane to lift the car, yet the country road was silent and deserted.

Then, all at once, the car was dropped. It fell with a crash. The girl on the back seat was flung against the top of the car. She had been too shocked to utter a sound before, but now she began howling with pain and terror. Brian was shaking as he turned the key in the ignition. The car started! He raced it down the dirt road back to Manistee.

Brian has never returned to Nagoon Park. And he no longer laughs at the tales told about it. He has his own story now.

The Portrait

A few years after World War I, a prominent Boston artist was a house guest in the home of a Mr. Izzard. He was given the best room in the old family mansion that stood on the outskirts of Boston. It was a large bedroom on the top floor with side windows that looked out on landscaped gardens.

The first night he was awakened suddenly by a brilliant glow that hurt his eyes and made his flesh crawl. In that light he saw a woman in an elegant gown standing at the side of the room. Fascinated, he watched as she hurled something out of the window. He couldn't see what it was.

Then the woman turned around and looked at him. She would have been beautiful if her face had not been set in such hard, cruel lines. Dark, malignant eyes flashed their hatred. Her lips were pursed in a smirk of triumph. As that gloating face stared at him, the light and figure slowly faded and disappeared.

The next two nights the horrible vision repeated itself. After the third appearance, the artist felt compelled to sketch the face of the woman he had seen. Later he showed the drawing to his city friends. Everyone was disturbed by the evil in it.

Several months later, Mr. Izzard again invited the artist to his home. This time he led his friend through a gallery of portraits of his ancestors.

The artist stopped suddenly before one of the paintings. It was the portrait of a beautiful and demure young woman.

"I've met her somewhere I'm sure," he exclaimed. "I'd know that face anywhere—only—"

Mr. Izzard laughed. "You couldn't have known her," he said. "She's been dead for a hundred years. She was my great-grandfather's second wife and she certainly was no credit to the family."

He went on to explain that his great-grandfather's first wife had died, leaving behind her little son. His second wife, having given birth to her own son, was filled with jealousy, sure the family property would go to the older boy. One day his crumpled body was found below the window of the bedroom where the artist had seen the vision. The child had died instantly of a broken neck.

"She was suspected of having murdered him," Mr. Izzard explained. "But nothing could ever be proved."

"It can now," the artist exclaimed. Describing what he had seen, he went to get the drawing he had made.

To his horror, Mr. Izzard saw that the features of the woman in the sketch were the exact features of the woman in the portrait.

Haunted Ferreby House

Sometimes greed reaches even beyond the grave. Perhaps this is what happened in the case of the mansion known as Hopsfield. It got its name because it stood in the middle of a field of hops outside the town of Waterlooville in Hampshire, England.

A huge, rambling Gothic-style house, it was built by a Ferreby in the early 1800s. Proud of his mansion, which boasted a long flight of stone steps to the front door, Mr. Ferreby was determined to have it stay in his family forever: It must never change hands. It would always be home to the Ferrebys. That was his dying wish.

The Ferreby offspring lived in the house and raised their children in it. But when the grandchildren were grown, and their parents had died, they wanted nothing to do with the old place. The rooms had always seemed dank and cold and the atmosphere was heavy and oppressive.

After moving out, the Ferrebys rented the house to a group of Spiritualists, who weren't there long before they began complaining that the ghost of old Mr. Ferreby kept appearing, shaking with anger and threatening them. They were so terrified that they asked for and received permission to sublet the house.

The new occupants were a widow and her daughter, then in her twenties. They stayed only a short while. The mother was found dead in her bed at one o'clock in the morning. Soon afterwards, the daughter moved out of the grim old house, which by this time had begun to get a sorry reputation.

No one else wanted to rent the house. But the Ferreby heirs were able to sell it. It was bought almost immediately by a newly retired sea captain and his wife. One of the captain's treasures was a collection of Indian daggers he had gathered on his travels. He now kept them in a display case in the hall of the Ferreby house.

One morning the sea captain was found lying dead in the front hall, one of his Indian daggers buried in his back. His widow moved out immediately, leaving behind a mystery that the police couldn't solve. Only the local people claimed to know what had happened: Old Ferreby's ghost, long in his uneasy grave, was the killer.

By this time no local person would think of going near the old house. But in the 1920s it caught the eye of the Dalton family, who were determined to buy it even against the advice of advisors and friends. The old Gothic-style building appealed to Mr. Dalton. The dark gloominess of its interior, he said, was the result of neglect. The rooms could be renovated and the atmosphere improved. He poured money into the house, transforming it into a beautiful and luxurious home, but he was never able to get rid of the strange chill that seemed to pervade it.

Overnight guests of the Daltons remember uneasy nights—strange noises, doors that were opened by invisible hands, children who woke in the middle of the night to find themselves crammed under their beds. And everyone still complained of the cold, oppressive atmosphere that no amount of renovations could change.

But there was no discussing these things with the Daltons. They had ready explanations: Children do strange things in their sleep; old houses settle at night, making noises of all kinds; doors come open under the pressure of drafts. The dank, chill atmosphere was just the psychological effect of all those scary stories.

Then one summer Dalton's son, a brilliant young man attending Oxford—with everything apparently going for him—went into the basement of the old house with a gun and blew out his brains. A few weeks later his grieving mother died. Not long after that Mr. Dalton himself suddenly dropped dead in his dressing room. Only one child remained, a daughter. She moved out at once. The magnificently renovated house was boarded up and left empty. No one went near it now. Cold and grim, it stood alone in the field of hops. Did old Mr. Ferreby have his wish at last?

Madness in the Museum

The Gothic-style building that houses the Fremantle Museum in Western Australia was built in 1863 by convicts as an asylum for the mentally ill. During its heyday it was crowded with these sufferers, among them some who were criminally insane.

In 1963, when the vacated buildings were turned into a museum and art center, the rooms were enlarged and modernized and used to display historical relics.

Despite the renovations, the ghosts of those who once lived and died here still seem to haunt the halls. Papers, mops and dusters are sometimes snatched from the hands of employees and tossed around the floor. Knocking is heard in the walls. Footsteps echo up and down the halls.

But the most terrifying things happen in the Discovery Gallery on the second floor. Its story is a dark one. It once contained a block of eight small cells in which violent patients were housed. One of the cells has been preserved to show how badly the criminally insane were treated in the past. The small, cramped cell is equipped with a heavy wooden door that was bolted from the outside.

One day in the late 1970s, a school teacher was taking a group of students through the museum. As she entered the Discovery Gallery, she suddenly began to shove, push and struggle as though she were being attacked by an unseen assailant. All the while she was unable to speak or to hear the questions of her terrified students. At last a museum official was able to lead the teacher out of the room.

The story of the teacher's experience came to the ears of a a brash young man who had just been hired by the museum and was visiting it for the first time. We'll call him Alan. He decided he would prove that there were no such things as ghosts by going to the Discovery Gallery and even entering the model cell. But he had no sooner entered the Gallery than he began gasping for breath. He raced down the stairs and out of the building, where he became violently ill.

Alan stayed away from the museum for two months claiming illness. When he returned, he was just as determined as ever to prove the Gallery had no ghosts. This time he was able to go only a short way up the stairs when he began gagging again. Scarcely able to catch his breath, he fled the building. Ghosts or no ghosts, Alan had finally had enough. He quit the job and never went back.

But the most terrifying example of the ghostly power in the Discovery Gallery took place the afternoon three schoolgirls drifted into it. When they came to the model cell, two of the girls pushed the third girl inside as a practical joke. They slammed the door shut on her and bolted it.

What followed, according to officials and visitors who were there, was an explosion of supernatural fury. With a roar, something like a great whirlwind came sweeping through, rattling doors and windows, snatching papers from tables and desks and sending them careening around the room. Through all this weird commotion came the ghastly screams of the hysterical girl in the cell.

Finally someone made it to the wooden door, slid back the bolt and led the girl out. At that moment the whirlwind died down. Doors and windows stopped rattling. Papers settled on the floor. Calm returned, but not to the girl. Sobbing and shaking uncontrollably, she tried to tell what had happened to her. But her voice came out a jumble of unintelligible words. It was her eyes, glassy with horror, that revealed something of what she had experienced, cooped up in that tiny cell with the raging ghost of a long-dead madman.

4. THE SPECTRES

- Was it a prehistoric bird, a lost species, a strange mutation . . . or was it something else?

- The next time you're in Ohai at night, make sure you don't visit Creek Road . . .

- A phantom horse brings its rider home . . .

- What is it that is trapped on Diamond Island?

- Horror is a puppy the size of a matchbox . . .

Mothman

Strange things sometimes happen that can turn a simple little event into a nightmare. On November 16, 1966, around 9 P.M., Mr. and Mrs. Raymond Wamsley invited their friend Marcella Bennett and her two-year-old daughter Tina to join them in a surprise visit to their friends the Thomases.

The Wamsleys lived in a little town in the West Virginia countryside. Ralph Thomas lived up the road in the midst of woodlands.

The Wamsley party drove down the dirt road towards their destination. On the way they had to pass an area formerly used by the army for storing explosives. The cement domes, or igloos, built to contain the explosives, were abandoned. They stood empty. The deserted place had an eerie feel about it. And as the Wamsleys drove by, they noticed a strange red light hovering over one of the igloos. Not having any idea what it was, Richard Wamsley stepped on the gas and sped away. Soon after, they reached the Thomas house, and parked in front.

Marcella Bennett was the first to jump out of the car, carrying her sleeping daughter. At that instant, a figure began to rise slowly behind the car. Marcella thought it must have been lying on the ground when it was disturbed by their arrival. Unable to move, she stared at it as it loomed before her. It was in the shape of a man, huge and grey with great wings folded on its back. And its large red eyes glowed in the dark.

Marcella collapsed, dropping her child, who screamed in pain and terror. The Wamsleys were as terrified as Marcella. They jumped out of the car and raced for the Thomas house. Behind them Marcella broke through the spell that she was under, snatched up Tina and rushed after them. They were let into the house by three of the Thomas children, who said their parents weren't home.

Ralph Wamsley locked the door behind them and made for the telephone. Excited by the hysteria of the older people, the children rushed to the window and looked out. They saw the strange grey monster shuffling onto the porch.

By the time the police arrived, the creature had disappeared. However, the Mothman, as it came to be called by the press, continued to make numerous appearances elsewhere in West Virginia. Throughout November, witnesses in five counties phoned law enforcement agencies to report sightings of the Mothman.

Richard West, who lived in Charleston, West Virginia, phoned on the evening of November 21 to describe a "Batman" that was sitting on the roof of a neighbor's home. The Batman, he said, must have been six feet (1.8m) tall, with a wing span of some six to eight feet (1.8–2.4m). Besides its great wings, the most distinguishing thing about it was its pair of huge red eyes.

On November 25, Thomas Ury, who was driving along Route 62 about 7:15 in the morning, phoned in to tell about a tall grey man standing in a nearby field. As he watched, the "man" spread a pair of huge wings and flew straight up like a helicopter. When it was about 150 feet (45m) above Ury's car, it began to circle over it. Ury, driving at 75 miles (120km) per hour could not shake the creature. He sped towards the only protection he could think of—Sheriff George Johnson at Point Pleasant. By the time he got there, the Mothman was gone. But Ury was so unnerved, he couldn't go to work that day.

On the evening of November 26, Mrs. Ruth Foster of St. Albans, West Virginia, phoned to say that the Mothman was standing on her front lawn beside the porch. It was tall and had a pinched face that didn't seem to have any other features except for huge red eyes that seemed to pop out of its head like the eyes of a crab.

At 10:30 on the Sunday morning of November 27, 18-year-old Connie Carpenter, who was driving home from church, came face to face with the Mothman, which almost caused her to have an accident.

That evening the Mothman returned to St. Albans and chased two young girls, 13-year-old Sheila Cain and her little sister, as they ran screaming for home.

These were only a few of the calls phoned in to law enforcement agencies about the Mothman. More than 100 were received by the time the month came to an end.

What was this Mothman? Where had it come from? People began putting forward all kinds of explanations. Perhaps the Mothman was a bird from prehistoric times. Perhaps it was some lost, now almost extinct, species of human being or a mutation caused by gases escaping from the isolated explosives area where it may have been making its home.

Scientists would have loved to examine that strange and terrifying creature. But they never got a chance. As suddenly as it had appeared, the Mothman disappeared, leaving behind no footprints, no droppings, no signs of its visit—only questions.

The Ghosts of Creek Road

Dark, lonely roads seem to attract ghosts. People claim to have seen a number of them along Creek Road, which winds through the wilderness outside the town of Ohai in Southern California. The road is spooky even in daylight with the interlocking branches of gnarled live oaks overshadowing it. It can be an eerie place after dark. That's when the ghosts come out.

The best known among them is the Charman. Nobody knows his real name. He's called Charman because his body is practically burned to a crisp. Those who have seen him say he's a horrible sight, with flesh peeling away from his bones. His blackened face is a grinning skull from which a few shreds of skin still hang. Some people claim that when he appears he brings with him the sweet stench of burning flesh.

The Charman's anger and pain seem to have accompanied him into death. He has a habit of lunging out of the darkness and attacking anyone walking alone down the quiet road. In 1950 a teenager went for a walk on Creek Road to prove his bravery and came rushing away white-faced, claiming that the Charman had torn his jacket from his back. His story made the papers.

There have been many theories about who the Charman really was. At first people thought he was a fireman who had burned to death in the 1948 fires that raged through the forests surrounding Ohai. Because his body was never found and given a decent burial, he was doomed to walk the shadowy road for all time, taking out his anger on innocent passersby.

This story was disproved when a look at old records showed that no firefighter had been lost in the fire of 1948. Then people said if not a forest fire, an automobile accident must have been the cause of the Charman's fiery death. A few have a much darker theory. They say the Charman could have been the victim of a murderer who torched him and left him to die in the forest. Now filled with rage, he stalks the dark road seeking revenge upon the man who killed him.

The Charman doesn't travel alone on dark, winding Creek Road. A young horsewoman has been seen there on the anniversary of her death. She rides reck-lessly down Creek Road until she reaches a place called the Curve, which is treacherously sharp. Here the horse stumbles, rears and throws her. She falls, breaks her neck and dies instantly. Then, in the next few minutes, she is back again, riding at breakneck speed to the killer curve. People say that she repeats this ride until day breaks and she can rest for another year.

A third ghost is the young bride who chooses the anniversary of her death to hitchhike down the old road in a white wedding dress stained with blood. No one knows who she was or why she was killed on her wedding day or why she chooses to hitchhike on this spooky road to commemorate the murder.

The fourth ghost in this strange assortment is a motorcyclist. He rides pell-mell down the treacherous road over and over again. It's hard to understand how he negotiates it so skillfully, because, you see, he has no head.

The Black Horse of Sutton

There are stories of phantom horses from all around the world. Usually, these horses are white or black. Sometimes they are never seen—only the clatter of their hooves is heard, along with the rattle of spurs and the smart crack-crack of the whip in the ghostly rider's hands. The horses gallop through history carrying important messages to kings and generals or their ladies.

The Black Horse of Sutton is unique in that it appeared only to a humble woman, old Mrs. Sutton.

She and her husband had established a homestead in the bush land outside the town of Goulburn in New South Wales, Australia. It was an isolated place removed many miles from the nearest human settlement. In that general area it was known as the Sutton Homestead, or just plain Sutton.

One spring day, Mr. Sutton had to ride into Goulburn to negotiate a land deal. He left Mrs. Sutton behind on the lonely homestead, promising to return as soon as possible. Those were the days when there were few roads. Transportation depended on the horse. Even the mail might take a month or more to arrive. Mrs. Sutton knew she might have a long wait before her.

Day by day, she waited eagerly for her husband's return. She had no way of knowing when he would be back, except by the sound of the hoofbeats of his returning horse. So one evening, a week after he left, when she heard the distant rat-a-tat-tat of galloping hooves, her heart leapt with happiness. She was sure that her husband was at last on his way home.

Closer and closer came the hoofbeats. They stopped at the outer gate. She heard the horse turning as if the rider were closing the gate behind him. Then came the click of the gate as it closed.

Now the thundering hoofbeats were galloping down the drive and around the corner of the house. Suddenly, a magnificent black stallion came into view. But, to Mrs. Sutton's horror, it was riderless. On hooves that hammered out a staccato beat, the horse galloped directly towards the shuddering woman. She cried out, terrified. But at the last minute the great beast shied away from her and trampled into the house, where it disappeared. The hoofbeats echoed in the ranges of distant mountains. Fainter and fainter they sounded until finally they disappeared altogether.

The next day a messenger arrived to tell Mrs. Sutton that on his way home the evening before, her husband had been thrown by his plodding farm horse. He had been found lying dead by the side of the road while the horse grazed quietly nearby.

Had the black stallion not been riderless after all? Was the soul of Mr. Sutton astride the horse—invisible but still present—as he rode home for the last time?

Twice more the spectre horse appeared to Mrs. Sutton. Once it came to announce the death of her elder son, killed in the Boer War in South Africa. Later, it came to tell her of her younger son's accidental death.

When old Mrs. Sutton died, the homestead she and her husband loved so much was demolished. Progress transformed it into a hamlet of small homes. Fine roads and automobiles linked the inhabitants to the outside world.

And the Black Horse of Sutton gallops no more.

Great Ball of Fire

Diamond Island lies in a river opposite the small hamlet of Hardin, Illinois. Early in 1888 people began talking about a mysterious ball of fire, the size of a large barrel, that appeared around midnight at the foot of the island and moved around—without, however, setting anything on fire. The light intrigued the people of Hardin so much that they would line the far shore every night to watch it as it drifted here and there before vanishing.

One night a group of young men decided to visit the island and investigate the mysterious light firsthand. Afraid it might be a dangerous smuggler or a thief of some kind, they armed themselves to the teeth for their adventure. Bristling with revolvers, knives, shotguns and clubs, they set out in a small skiff they had rented.

The men were in high spirits as they rowed to the island, landing at a point that was not far from the spot where the light made its nightly appearance. Here they hauled their skiff ashore, beaching it high above the waterline. Then they hid in a grove of trees and waited.

Darkness came down as the hours ticked by. Stars splattered the sky. Nothing unusual was seen or heard above the gentle ripple of the river. Then, just as they were wondering if the whole thing had been a hoax, the light appeared, rising out of the river at the south end of the island.

As it rose, it grew in intensity, flooding the whole area with a crimson light. Higher and higher it went, up, up, up, until it hovered 120 feet (36.5m) in the air. Then it faded away. And darkness seemed to return to the hushed island.

The young men had seen enough. All they wanted now was to escape the island. They rushed for their boat. But as they reached the edge of the shore, they stopped, horrified. The little skiff was already moving out. It seemed to be propelled by the ball of red fire— which was now perched in it!

As the men watched in growing panic, the crimson ball took the shape of a man. He was pulling steadily on the oars, sending the skiff into midstream. His face was hidden under the wide brim of a floppy hat, but the rest of him could be seen quite plainly, because the boat and the waters and air that surrounded him were lit up by the weird brightness.

The young men stood in shocked silence, paralyzed with fear, their eyes fastened on the boat with its ghastly occupant, who was moving farther and farther away. It was as though whoever the spectre was, he was desperately trying to escape the island. But before he could reach the far shore, he changed again into a fiery ball. Slowly it rose from the boat, climbing into the sky, until at treetop level it disappeared. Black night descended once more on the island. Across the river, the lights of Hardin twinkled.

It was as though the young men on the island were released from a binding spell. They began shouting for help at the tops of their voices. At last, a fisherman sleeping on the far shore launched his own boat, pulled across to the island and rescued them.

The fiery ghost continued to make its nightly visits to the island. But neither the young men nor anyone else cared to investigate it again. The people of Hardin were quite willing to accept the only explanation available. Several years before, a man had been betrayed and brutally murdered on the island. The great ball of fire was his restless ghost.

The Expanding Dog

Several years ago, when I visited the Chumash Indian reservation in the Santa Ynez valley, I met an elderly woman known to her friends as Aunt Minnie. She told me about a very strange experience she had one night when walking home from a visit with a friend.

It was a pleasant summer evening with a young moon riding low in the east. Suddenly, Aunt Minnie heard a whispering sound behind her. At first she thought it was a breeze rustling the leaves of the live oaks. But when she looked up, she saw nothing stirring. She turned around to find out if something was following her. She saw a tiny puppy trotting along behind her.

It didn't look dangerous, but there was something very strange about it. It was no larger than a small matchbox! Whoever heard of a dog that small?

Aunt Minnie quickened her steps, just wanting to get home. But the whispering sound continued to pursue her, and it kept growing louder. She looked back again.

The puppy had grown. It was much larger now, the size of a big cat. A real dog couldn't grow that fast, she thought. Aunt Minnie began to run, but always behind her came the whispering, whispering. She kept glancing over her shoulder—and every time she looked, the dog was bigger, and it was close on her heels.

By the time she reached the gate of her home, the dog was almost as large as a pony and had turned jet black. Huge red eyes glared at her. Fangs gleamed white in slavering, open jaws. Aunt Minnie's knees were so wobbly she could hardly walk. Somehow she managed to push through the gate, stagger to her front door, open it and collapse inside.

Her husband, Ben, helped her to a chair. She sat, pale and shivering, unable to say a word. Ben got a blanket and wrapped her up in it, but she still went on shaking and her teeth were chattering. At last she managed to tell Ben about the dog.

Ben grabbed his gun and ran out to shoot the creature, but it had disappeared. He could hear its faint baying in the hushed night—a ghostly baying that he realized could only come from a ghost dog.

"That's what it was," he told me, "a ghost dog with a ghost shaman for its master. It's been seen by others around here since. We know where it comes from— that old graveyard where the shamans did their black magic.

"No use to shoot at it. I just put my gun away. And told my Minnie she was plenty lucky to get away so quick inside."

5. THE SEARCHERS

- Who is the man in the bowler hat who haunts Runway No. 1 at Heathrow? And why does he keep coming back?

- A forlorn young woman, she is eternally seeking a ride home . . .

- Do ghosts have pets? This one does!

- A grieving phantom seeks her long-lost daughter—does she find her at last?

The Man in the Bowler Hat

England's Heathrow Airport is noted for its ghosts. Perhaps the most persistent of them is the apparition that appears on Runway No. 1.

It all began back in 1948 when a DC3 Dakota owned by Sabena Belgian Airways tried to make a landing on Runway No. 1 in thick fog and crashed, killing all 22 passengers and crew. The plane burst into flames upon impact.

Airport personnel had just begun sifting through the wreckage when one by one they were interrupted by a man in a dark suit and a bowler hat. He had the same question for everyone:

"Excuse me, have you found my briefcase?"

It was only later at the conference held to determine the cause of the crash that the odd character was noted. Everyone remembered his approaching them with the question and each one thought it rather peculiar. As they discussed it, they began realizing how truly strange it was. The bodies of all the passengers and crew had been identified. None had survived. Then who was the man in the bowler hat?

Some 22 years later, in 1970, this question was asked by a police patrol that was cruising around the airport about one o'clock in the afternoon. A radio call came in, saying that a man in a bowler hat was seen on Runway No. 1. Off raced the police car. But the runway was empty and the police, saying, "False alarm," left. Less than an hour later, they received another call and raced back, only to find the runway still empty. As the afternoon slipped into dusk, the reports of a man in a bowler hat became more frequent. Finally, the control tower got into the act. Something was now appearing on the radar screen—a blip that was moving so slowly it had to be a human being.

This time police and airport personnel were determined to locate the trespasser on Runway No. 1. Three police cars drove side by side down the runway. No way could any human being evade them. Their headlights lit up the runway. It stretched away, empty and silent, before them.

But they had no sooner left the runway than more sightings were phoned in. This time the three police cars were joined by the airport fire engine on which a searchlight was mounted. The next time the control tower picked up the blip on its radar screen, it sent the three police cars and the fire engine racing back to Runway No. 1. Orders came to drive west.

The cars went with doused lights until they were

some thirty yards (27m) from the spot where the tower had located the blip. Then they switched on their headlights and searchlight and Runway No. 1 sprang into glaring brightness, empty and silent as before. They inched forward while messages poured in over the radio.

"You're ten yards away now.

"Five yards.

"Four yards.

"Three yards.

"Two yards . . ."

This was followed by a frantic order: "Stop! Whatever it is you've run over it!"

Police and firemen jammed on their brakes and spilled out of the cars and fire engine to look around. Again they found nothing. As before, Runway No. 1 was empty.

A voice crackled over the radio. "You must have missed him. He's walking away from you in the opposite direction. He's behind you now."

The police looked behind them and saw nothing. They drove slowly back. Wearily, they gave up their wild-goose chase, leaving the man in the bowler hat to continue his amble up and down the runway.

What could have been the life and death secret in that lost briefcase that would keep the man in the bowler hat relentlessly searching for it 22 years later?

The Girl from Leigh Park

Outside Waterlooville, England, there's a stretch of road without sidewalks. It's quite dangerous for pedestrians and few are seen on it, especially after nightfall.

On a November evening in 1976, Robert Spensley and his wife, who was at the wheel, were heading for home. As they reached the dangerous stretch of road, Spensley suddenly saw a girl in the fading light. She was standing directly in the path of the car and his wife was driving straight towards her. He yelled at her to stop or to swerve to miss the girl.

Mrs. Spensley gave her husband a peculiar look and went on driving. Her husband put his hands over his eyes and waited for the thud of impact. There was nothing. When he dared look again, the girl was gone. His wife was still driving calmly. She had seen nothing.

The next morning Spensley reported his strange experience to his co-workers. Several of them spoke up. They had also seen the girl on the road. They said that it was believed to be the ghost of a girl who had once lived in nearby Leigh Park. One evening, while trying to hitch a ride home, she had been struck down by a car and killed. Since that time, she had been seen by a number of motorists on the same stretch of road.

One of Spensley's friends had an even stranger story to tell about the girl from Leigh Park. He said he was driving home through a heavy rain when, as he passed the cemetery, he was flagged down by a young girl. She was wet through, bedraggled and very forlorn. She told him that she lived in Leigh Park and needed a lift there. He opened the door for her and she climbed in. She gave him the address in Leigh Park, but after that little was said by either of them. In the pouring rain, he had to keep his eyes and all his attention on the road. Finally he was in Leigh Park at the address the girl had given him.

"Here we are," he said, bringing the car to a stop. He reached over to open the car door for the girl when, to his shock, he saw that the seat was empty. The girl was gone, though the door was still shut and the window rolled up. For a second, he wondered if she had ever really been there.

Then he looked down at the seat where she had been sitting. It was sopping wet.

The Stuffed Dog

Priory House stands on the Isle of Wight, part of the British Isles. A lovely old house, it is called "Priory" because it was built on the foundations of what was once a Chinese monastery. Something of the peaceful atmosphere of the monastery seems to pervade the old house. Something also haunts it—the ghost of a young girl.

Her portrait hangs in the dining room. It shows a 14- or 15-year-old sitting on a garden seat. She is dressed in a long, blue gown in the style of the early 1700s. A satin ribbon fastens a little canary to her wrist. At her feet lies a small furry dog, a King Charles spaniel. The young girl must have lived in the house at one time, but so long ago that nobody remembers who she was.

Girl and canary have gone to their graves. But the dog remains. Stuffed, he sits in a glass case that is set over the main staircase. From there he surveys the rooms of Priory House with a penetrating stare whenever the light hits his glass eyes.

As for the Little Lady in Blue, as she came to be called, the grave couldn't hold her. She has been seen several times, a faint shadowy figure either on the staircase or in the gardens. She comes with a whiff of lavender perfume, bringing a breath of happiness, a light suggestion of tinkling laughter, the soft swish of silken skirts, and the faint patter of light footsteps as she skips at play.

For many years, the house was occupied by old Miss Laura, who cherished it. Most especially she felt a deep affection for the Little Lady in Blue, that gentle, happy ghost.

Then Miss Laura died. Since she left no heirs, the house was sold by the estate to a wealthy American woman. The new owner poured money into renovations. Most of the old furniture was sold. In its place antiques from different historical periods were bought and the rooms redecorated. The portrait of the Little Lady in Blue stayed. The dog in its glass case went. Finally the American moved in with a large staff of servants and the tranquil atmosphere of the old house was gone.

Now the servants were wakened at night by the sound of a child's feet clattering down the corridors, a child's voice crying between heartrending sobs, "Where is my dog? My little dog, where is he? I want my dog!"

The servants were distracted. One by one, they left. Last to go was the butler, who had worked for the American woman for many years. He told his employer unhappily that he could no longer bear the noises that were setting his nerves on edge.

Something had to be done, but what? Perhaps friends of old Miss Laura would know the answer. The American invited two of them for tea one day and plied them with questions. Why was a child racketing through the halls crying for her dog? What dog?

That was when they told her about the little stuffed dog in the glass case, the stuffed dog that was disposed of when the house was sold. Where was it now?

The American woman was nothing if not determined. She sent out tracers for the little dog, leaving no clue unchecked. Finally she found it in an antique shop in a town miles away. She bought it and returned it to its place above the stairwell. With its return, the noises stopped. Once more there was only the occasional patter of happy feet, a child's light tinkle of laughter, the soft swish of silk passing down the halls, contented sounds that troubled no one.

The American woman has long since sold the Priory. It was bought by a travel organization that had no trouble booking guests who were attracted by the Priory's quaint loveliness, its tranquil atmosphere and, most especially, by the stories of the happy little ghost. Hundreds passed through the old house.

Now and then management changed. But each manager who arrived to take over the job was given a stern warning:

"Whatever else you do, if you want to keep the peace here, never, never remove the stuffed dog in the glass case from its spot over the stairwell."

Where Is My Daughter?

One of the saddest ghosts I've heard of was that of an elderly woman. Back in the 1800s she and her husband had come from Ireland to Australia, where they settled on the west coast near the town of Fremantle. Widowed early, the woman had a beautiful young daughter with red hair and a sweet Irish face. One day her daughter was abducted.

The mother searched for the lost girl frantically until, wild with grief, she went insane and was locked up in the gloomy buildings that made up the asylum at Fremantle. She wandered the halls of her prison hospital, still searching. Then one day she ended her life by throwing herself out of a first-story window that was more than ten feet (3m) above the rocky ground. But her spirit still could not rest. Even after the asylum buildings were renovated to house a museum and an adjacent art center, the old woman continued to haunt their halls, searching for her lost daughter.

A number of people have come face to face with her—a frail wraith that vanished before their eyes. She always wore the same thing—a plain black dress with a white collar and lace frills down the front. A delicate Victorian-style cap framed her face.

Museum employees working late at night reported seeing her, lit by the ghostly lantern she carried, gliding noiselessly through the darkened corridors. And teachers grading papers late at night in their schoolrooms at the local high school would look down to see a flickering light moving from window to window of the old buildings. And they would whisper to one another that the poor woman was walking again.

Then, on March 19, 1980, Shelley, a young college student, came to the asylum to fulfill an assignment for her photography class. She was to shoot the various rooms of the art center. In one room, trying for an interesting shot, she turned her camera towards the windows. Through the lens she saw, peering back at her, the demented face of an elderly woman in a lace cap. The window in which the face appeared was more than ten feet (3m) above ground level—too high for anyone to play such an elaborate hoax.

Shelley thought at first it might have been just her imagination. But when she had the film developed, there was the face, just as she had seen it through her camera lens.

Shelley's photo was published in the local newspaper and created quite a stir. Photographers of all kinds flocked to the art center in hopes of capturing the old woman's image on film again. None were successful.

In the years that followed, the old woman's wispy figure was no longer seen in the halls of the old asylum. At night the windows were no longer illuminated by the flickering light of her lantern. Why?

Could it be that, looking through the window into the face of the girl behind the camera, she thought she had found her long-lost daughter at last? For Shelley is an Irish girl with beautiful red hair and dancing Irish eyes.

6. THE VIOLENT ONES

- A night in Room 310 could mean your death . . .

- A phantom strangler awaits a child in a "charming little room" . . .

- A violent spirit ties an entire household in knots . . .

- A haunt of ghosts almost becomes her grave too . . .

The Evil in Room 310

Marsha Bennett told me this story herself. She had been north to visit friends in the state of Washington. Now she was driving back to her home in California. The last lap of the day's journey was over the Cascade range that stretches from Washington to California. It was late evening and snow had begun to fall before she finally reached the little Oregon town where she planned to spend the night.

Tired and ready for a hot meal and a good night's sleep, she stopped at the first place she came upon. It was an old hotel on the main street. The lobby had a musty odor. The seedy clerk behind the desk signed her in. Her room was on the third floor—Room 310. An elderly bellhop helped her with her luggage.

As soon as the door was opened, a blast of hot air struck Marsha full in the face. With the hot air came something else, something she could not define but that filled her with dread. It was heavy and depressing, she explained, "with the strong scent of evil." She felt as if she was about to faint.

All she said was, "It's awfully hot."

The bellhop tinkered with the radiator knobs. Then he opened the window and left. The room began to cool off, but the feeling of despair and dread grew stronger. It centered on the open square of black window space. The terror seemed to speak in her mind.

"Go to the window," it said. "Throw yourself out, out out!"

Terrified, Marsha flung herself on the bed farthest from the window.

"I kept saying no, no, no to that voice," she told me, "but the voice kept insisting."

"You can't fight me, you puny thing," it said. "Sooner or later you'll jump. I'll make you! Jump! Jump! Jump!"

At last Marsha could stand it no longer. She jumped up, calling herself a coward.

"Coward or not," she explained, "I was sure that if I stayed the night, I'd be dead by morning."

Marsha was prepared to sacrifice the money she'd already paid just to leave, but when she went downstairs with her baggage to check out, the clerk never asked what was wrong or if she wished to try another room. He returned the full cash amount to her.

Marsha drove down the street to a modern motel. As she entered the lobby, she felt the dark depression slip from her shoulders. She became almost giddy with relief. She had planned to be on her way early the next morning. Instead she decided to stay over a day and look into the history of the old hotel to see if she could discover the reason for her terrifying experience there.

She visited the local library to make a few inquiries. An elderly librarian sat behind the desk.

"I'm just wondering," Marsha said tentatively. "Did anything shocking ever happen in the old hotel?"

The librarian looked at her strangely. "How did you come upon that bit of history?" she asked. "It took the hotel a long time to squash the story."

The librarian went on to tell what had happened. One evening back in 1948 a couple checked into the hotel as Mr. and Mrs. Oscar Smith. The next morning hotel employees found the young woman's body lying on the sidewalk outside the hotel beneath Room 310. The man who had registered as her husband had disappeared.

"At first it was ruled suicide," the librarian concluded. "But then they pried open her fist and found it clutched a handful of dark curly hair, not her own. So they made a search for the murderer. But he was never found . . .

"By the way," the librarian suddenly added, "isn't that a coincidence! It all happened on November 5th, 40 years ago yesterday."

Gas Brackets

Eileen Nye, who has since moved to Australia, tells this frightening story of an incident that took place during her days in England. When her work took her to a small English village, Eileen was delighted. It was quiet and peaceful, a perfect place in which to bring up her eight-year-old daughter.

Eileen found a delightful old gabled house, rented it at once and moved in with her daughter. She chose a charming little room for the child. Though it now had electric lights, it once had been lighted by gas. The old brass brackets still decorated its walls, adding a quaint old-fashioned touch to the room.

Mother and daughter settled into their new home, adjusting easily to the village life. There was just one flaw. A few days after they moved in, the little girl began complaining of a sore throat.

Then one night Eileen woke up to muffled screams coming from her daughter's room. She rushed in and found the child sitting upright in bed, clutching her throat with one hand and pointing with the other to something in the corner of the room. Eileen couldn't see anything there. When the child tried to explain, only garbled sounds came out.

The next day Eileen took the little girl to the village doctor, who couldn't find anything physically wrong, except for one peculiar fact: there were marks on her throat that looked like thumb prints.

That night, something told Eileen to check on her daughter, though she had heard nothing. When she went into the room, the child seemed to be sleeping peacefully. But there was something strange that made Eileen come to the bedside to get a closer look. The little girl's eyes were wide open. She wasn't sleeping— she was unconscious!

Eileen rushed her daughter to the doctor, who admitted the child to a nearby hospital for treatment and observation. Perhaps, he suggested to Eileen, the key to the child's condition might not lie in a physical ailment but in the past of the old house. Why not check into its history?

Eileen followed his advice. She was horrified to discover that a former tenant, now dead, had strangled his wife in the bedroom Eileen's daughter was using. He had then hung the body from one of the brass brackets, perhaps to make it look like a suicide.

Eileen moved out of the house at once and her daughter recovered completely. But the village doctor believes she had a narrow escape in the old house. It's his opinion that if she had stayed in that room another night, she would surely have died at the ghostly hands of a dead strangler.

Vicious Knots

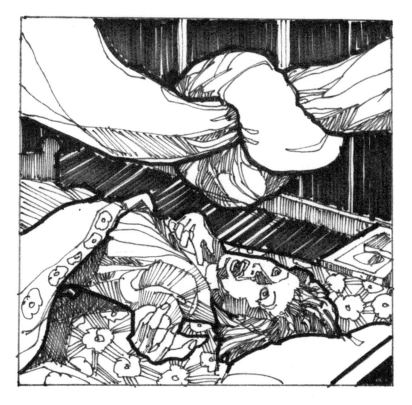

One day in 1928 Mrs. Sims went to visit her family, who lived in Montreal, Canada. The family consisted of her parents, two older sisters, two younger brothers and a beautiful teenage sister. When Mrs. Sims arrived, she found something strange was going on.

Knots were appearing mysteriously throughout the house.

There were knots in the window curtains and knots in the clothes hanging in the closets. The knots had first appeared in a back room where the teenager stayed. From there they had spread to other downstairs rooms. Then they began appearing upstairs. Soon knots showed up in the mother's best dresses. They were tied so tightly that many of her clothes were ruined. Mrs. Sims decided to stay and help her family through this strange crisis.

As the days passed, more and more peculiar things began to happen. One night, when Mrs. Sims and her parents were in the house alone, they started walking down the long hall to the living room when they stopped short. The thick drapes that usually hung in the hallway had been gathered up and tied together. Several heavy overcoats had been woven into them to form a gigantic tangled knot that hung three feet above the floor. An umbrella thrust into the knot pointed skyward like an exclamation point. Mrs. Sims gasped and then ran screaming from the house. It was several hours before she found the courage to return.

Two days later, something even more frightening happened. Mrs. Sims' mother woke in the middle of the night to find that the top blanket had been ripped off her bed and tied in a huge knot. It hung directly over her face, as if it were preparing to smother her. It seemed that the knots were becoming deadly now.

By this time, word of the knots was spreading. Visitors began flocking to the house—Spiritualists, reporters, two detectives from the police department. The detectives searched the house. They found a foul stench in the basement—a stench the family said they had never smelled before. Bloodhounds were brought in to sniff out a possible murder victim. No victim was found.

Finally, the detectives asked each person in the family to tie a knot. The youngest daughter was the only one to tie the intricate kind of knot that had been appearing all over the house. It seemed as though she was the one responsible. But, if so, how could she have done it when even muscular adults couldn't have handled those heavy drapes in the hall? And how could she have made the knots appear when she wasn't even home?

The knot-tying went on for six weeks. Then one day the teenager summoned her mother and one of her older sisters to her room. As the door opened to let them in, Mrs. Sims saw the curtains blowing wildly— though the windows were closed. The room itself seemed to brim with an eerie force.

Mrs. Sims waited outside the room for what seemed like a long while. Finally, her mother came out. Her grim face was white and her eyes were sick with horror and fear. But she never said a word. Neither she nor her daughters ever spoke about what took place in that room that day, when she grappled with the force that had been terrorizing the household. However, from then on, the knot-tying stopped and the family returned to its former normal routines.

What price did Mrs. Sims' mother have to pay when she bartered for the peace of her family in that closed-off room? Only three people know the answer to that.

Evil Hands

During the time that Amanda was a member of the staff on Quarantine Station, she often said she wasn't afraid of the ghosts that people claimed to have seen there. She wasn't afraid, that is, until the night one tried to kill her.

Back in Colonial times, the Station was established on the rocky North Point of Manly Peninsula, a suburb of Sydney, Australia. When epidemics broke out on ships bringing immigrants to Australia, everyone aboard was quarantined at Manly Cove until the danger of contagion was past. Few survived the quarantine period.

Today Quarantine Station is a national park. The old whitewashed buildings used as hospital and isolation wards have been preserved as landmarks. But something else seems to have survived, too—the ghosts of those who died here. So many sightings have been reported that guides regularly conduct ghost tours through the sprawling grounds.

Whether anyone sees a ghost or not, almost everyone admits to feeling the eerie atmosphere that settles upon Quarantine Station after dark. The spell is so strong that even members of the staff make sure to leave with the last tour group every night.

Only Amanda chose to remain. She couldn't imagine why anyone should fear the spirits of the gentle, suffering settlers who were buried here, and she loved the lonely beauty of the grounds. She was so confident of her safety that she made one of the isolation wards her living quarters, spending nights as well as days in it.

Then, one horrifying night of bright moonlight, everything changed. Amanda went for a walk along the coastal cliffs that fall away from the headlands on which Quarantine Station stands. She lingered there, revelling in the silence, gazing across the dark harbor at the lights of Sydney, as the moonlight spread its mysterious web over the dreaming land and sea.

All at once her mood was shattered. A presence hot and evil seemed to be pressing close against her. Strong hands suddenly struck her in the middle of her back. They began shoving her forward with tremendous force.

Amanda's feet scrabbled on the rocky cliff edge as she fought to regain her balance. Far below she could see the white line of surf breaking silver against the rocks. She knew that if she went down she would be bashed to death on those rocks. She had to get free. But no matter how hard she struggled, she couldn't break away from the thing that was pushing her so relentlessly forward.

Now her feet were beginning to slide over the brink. Pebbles were being dislodged. She could hear the clattering of the stones on the rocks below and knew she was about to follow them. She was down to her last chance.

Gathering up all the strength she had, Amanda flung herself backwards. The cruel hands loosened, their force spent. Amanda whirled around to see who was there. There was nothing! Everything was quiet and hushed as before.

Terrified, Amanda fled back along the footpath that had seemed so friendly only minutes before. She stumbled and fell and got up again and ran, gasping, all the way until she reached the safety—would it ever be safe again?—of the isolation ward.

Early the next day she resigned from her job and left Quarantine Station forever. Those invisible, cruel hands had reminded her of something she had forgotten. The first shipload of passengers to be detained at Quarantine Station had been convicts—and some among them had been violent criminals.

7. THE GUARDIANS

- Prayer from Norway protects Liv Ullmann in London . . .

- Who was it that came to the old house at ten o'clock every night?

- Where did the creature with the huge glittering eyes come from? And what did it want?

- What is the Fourth Presence?

A Call for Help

Seventeen-year-old Liv Ullmann was in London for the first time. The beautiful Norwegian actress had spent most of her childhood in the little town of Trondhage, Norway. Her widowed mother supported herself and her child with the proceeds from a small dress shop she owned.

From the time she was small, Liv had always wanted to be an actress. When she reached her 17th birthday, her mother sent her to London to study drama under actress Irene Brent. Liv stayed at the London Y.W.C.A. Outside the security of that rooming house, London glittered with fascinating sights. The girl saw nothing there to threaten her, for she judged the big city by the experiences she had had in her hometown, where everyone was always friendly and everyone—even strangers—could be trusted.

One afternoon, about five o'clock, Liv and a friend were walking along a London street when a limousine slowed and then stopped beside them. A kindly-looking, well-dressed man leaned out the car window and asked the girls if they wanted a ride home.

Back in Norway, they had often accepted rides from fellow Norwegians whom they didn't know. So they climbed into the limousine without thinking. As soon as they were in the back seat, the man pushed a switch that locked all the doors automatically. He also shut and locked the sliding glass window that separated him from the girls. They found themselves in a tight little prison from which there was no escape.

Too late Liv remembered the stories she'd read in the London newspapers about girls who were kidnapped to be sold into slavery in foreign lands. Terrified, the teenagers struggled to open the doors. They pounded on the glass window that separated them from the driver. The man in the front seat paid no attention to their struggles and screams.

Finally, Liv stopped struggling and began to pray. She thought of her mother in faraway Norway, her mother who had always been there to protect her. She folded her hands and sent out a silent plea.

"Mother, mother," she whispered, "Help! Help me!"

Shortly afterwards, the car slowed down.

The girls held their breath.

The man in the front seat slid back the window that separated him from the girls.

"Where do you live?" he asked.

When they told him, he drove to the Y.W.C.A., unlocked the doors and swung them open. As the girls scrambled out, he said, "Well, maybe you've learned a lesson."

It seemed to the teenagers that they had been in that terrible car for ages. But when Liv looked at her watch, she was surprised to see how little time had gone by. It was only five minutes past five.

The next week Liv got a letter from her mother.

"Please tell me what you were doing last Wednesday afternoon," her mother wrote. "I was in the shop when suddenly an overwhelming fear for you forced me to go to the back room. There I fell to my knees and I folded my hands and I prayed for your life and your safety as I have never prayed before. It was just five minutes past five when I felt the dark cloud lift and I could go back to work."

Liv says her mother never had had a psychic experience before. But the bond between them is so strong that she was able to pick up her daughter's desperate cry for help. Liv is sure that it was her mother's fervent prayer fueled by love that was able to soften the mind of a hardened criminal many miles away.

Footsteps

A practical nurse, Phyllis Hudson has met a lot of odd people in very unusual circumstances. One of the strangest cases occurred in an old house in Westcott, near Darling, England.

The house stood in the center of what was once a rose garden, the pride of the neighborhood. The bushes, tended by the owner of the house, had been covered with luxuriant blooms. But since he died two years before, the garden had grown to weeds and it was too much for his widow to handle.

When the widow herself became seriously ill and was confined to bed, she required 24-hour care, so

Mrs. Hudson was hired as a live-in nurse.

The widow's bedroom was on the second floor of the rambling two-story house. At first Mrs. Hudson slept in a small bedroom next to her charge. But she soon changed to a room at the opposite end of the house. The reason Mrs. Hudson changed rooms also kept relatives away from night visits to the widow. After seven P.M. no one came to see her, no matter how many might arrive during daylight hours.

The reason was the footsteps. At ten o'clock every night footsteps would be heard at the front door. Slowly, deliberately, they would cross the hall to the stairs and then start mounting them steadily.

At first, Mrs. Hudson thought it was an intruder. She stood at the head of the stairs and watched anxiously. But though she could hear the footsteps mounting higher and higher, she saw no one. She might have laid it all down to imagination, except for the family dog. When the footsteps started climbing upwards he would sit beside her at the top of the stairs, cowering, the thick ruff of hair on the back of his neck standing upright, a growl deep in his throat. He was obviously terrified.

As the footsteps came towards her, Mrs. Hudson could no longer stand her ground. She would back away from the stairs and hurry down the hall to her own room. With a final yap, the dog would follow her, tail between his legs.

The footsteps would reach the upper landing and go into the widow's bedroom. The only one not upset by the footsteps was the old woman herself, who said the invisible visitor was just her husband coming to make his nightly call.

One day the widow died, and from that moment the footsteps no longer sounded in the silent house. But to everyone's amazement, the dilapidated rose garden suddenly burst into huge fragrant blossoms more beautiful than anyone could remember having seen before.

People around there said it was the husband's way of giving his wife a royal welcome.

Dreamtime Visitor

An Aboriginal family living in a small town in South Australia went on a camping trip in the Coorong. The Coorong is a coastal strip of swamp and dunes about 87 miles (140km) long. Low tide along the Coorong exposes wide expanses of salt flats. That night the Aboriginal family was out spotlighting on the flats. To spotlight, they shone their powerful hand-held flashlights across the flats to pick up crabs and other sea creatures.

All at once, the powerful lights illuminated a trail of giant footprints crossing the muck. They were spaced about four feet (1.2m) apart. The Aborigines looked out over the flats to see what had made the tracks, and found themselves staring into two shining eyes the size of automobile headlights, and they were spaced almost the same distance apart. But their eerie sheen was unlike any car lights the Aborigines had ever seen. As they looked into the huge eyes, the terrified family felt a strange tingling sensation travelling through their bodies, like an electric charge. They turned and fled.

At first the non-Aboriginal neighbors of the family scoffed at the story, calling it a wild fairy tale. Then some of those neighbors went camping on the Coorong and saw for themselves the great eyes staring at them and felt the same electric chill of fear. Other reports began to filter in.

One came from Cooberpedy, some 700 miles (1127 km) to the north of the Coorong. Cooberpedy is a little opal-mining town in Australia's inland desert region where rainfall averages less than three inches (8cm) a year. Only the hardiest desert growths can exist there. Most large creatures would find it difficult to survive.

There aren't many homes above ground in Cooberpedy. People use bulldozers to dig cave homes in the low hills that surround the town. These homes are beautifully furnished and quite comfortable. Josh and his family live in one of them. Sometimes he and his neighbors get together for an evening of bridge.

One night the bridge players were gathered in Josh's home, a game in progress. Suddenly Josh felt a tingling like a strong electric charge run through his body. The hair on his arms stood up. His scalp crawled. He jumped to his feet and ran to the front door. Flinging it open, he stepped outside.

The sky above him was velvet black, sparkling with desert stars against which the humps of hills rose in scallops. Then he turned to see two great luminous eyes staring down upon him from the summit of the hill at whose base he stood. The eyes were set about four feet (1.2m) apart, and there was a strange glitter in them. Josh had seen that glow before. It was the same glitter that appeared in the eyes of his cat when it was stalking a mouse.

Shaking with terror, Josh slammed the door shut and told his neighbors what he had seen. But, by the time they rushed out to get a look at the eyes, the creature had disappeared.

What animal has such huge, piercing eyes? None in this world that we know of, that's certain. But the Aborigines have an answer.

"They're our animal ancestors, the dreamtime heroes," they explain. "We use secret rituals to enter the dreamtime in which they still live. So why can't they leave the dreamtime to visit us? And when they do, better watch out. Some of those fellas can be pretty fierce and mean, if you make them mad."

The Fourth Presence

When Sir Ernest Shackleton wrote a book about his experiences in Antarctica, he mentioned a Fourth Presence that had once saved his life. It began in 1914 when Shackleton embarked on an ambitious plan to cross Antarctica by way of the South Pole.

The expedition, the second he had made to the frozen continent, was jinxed from the start. He had hoped that the Weddell Sea off the coast of Antarctica would be navigable. Instead, unseasonable weather had broken up the firm sheet of ice that usually, at this time of year, lined the coast. Now smaller sheets of ice (ice floes) of all shapes and sizes along with icebergs filled the bay. They crashed and ground against each other as storms roiled the waters below. Shackleton's ship was imprisoned in this churning jumble of ice blocks, and then it was crushed. On November 21st, it sank, leaving the 28-man crew to survive as best it could on the ice floes.

It was the following April before there was sufficient open water to launch the three small boats the men had brought with them from their sinking ship. On these boats they made their way to isolated Elephant Island, which provided shelter, but little else. There was no chance of rescue from the island because ships bypassed it.

Shackleton decided to make his way to the island of South Georgia, where there was a large whaling station. Two of the three boats were too small to make the more than 800-mile (1280km) journey there. Shackleton chose six men to accompany him in the largest boat.

It took 16 days for them to reach King Haakon Bay on South Georgia. Enclosed by tall, rugged cliffs, the harbor was almost as isolated as Elephant Island. The men would have to get to the opposite side of South Georgia, where the whaling station was located.

The boat in which they had come was so battered by storms and high seas that Shackleton was afraid it would never make the trip. Land passage was the only way, even though he knew the interior of the island was a gigantic death trap. No one had ever been able to cross it before.

Shackleton chose two able men, Worsley and Crean, to accompany him. They planned to travel light, taking only three days' rations, a primus lamp filled with oil, a small cooker, a few matches, an adze that could be used as an ice axe, and a 50-foot (15m) long alpine rope. Though it was bitter cold, they left their sleeping bags behind, because the weight would have slowed them down.

The trio set out at three o'clock in the morning. The sky was clear with a full moon shining. By its light the men threaded a path around the glacier that spilled down the cliffs into Haakon Bay. It took them two hours to climb 2500 feet (962m). From there they could look out on a mass of high peaks fronted by perpendicular cliffs. Steep snow slopes fell away in all directions. The frozen rivers of ancient glaciers glimmered in the moonlight.

Swallowing their fear, the men set off through the forbidding, frigid world. As they tramped through soft snow, Shackleton suddenly felt a fourth presence, invisible but real, walking at his side. During the long, harrowing trek, the presence stayed with him. It was there when blinding fogs blanketed everything. It seemed to give him strength as, dangling from the rope, he chiselled steps in a glacier's steep slope for the men to follow. It built up his resolve when, time after time, he found himself going in the wrong direction and had to lead his men back along the hazardous way they had come. It was there, too, a protector and guide, as the three picked their way through mazes of dangerous crevasses, half concealed by snow.

On the second night, exhausted, half frozen, despairing, the men had to force themselves to trudge on under the cold moon. They didn't dare stop for sleep, because without their warm bags, sleep would end in death. Through the long hours, the presence continued to stay with them, lending courage and strength.

Finally, 36 hours after they had set out from King Haakon Bay, the men achieved the impossible. They reached the shore and the whaling station without any loss of life or serious injury. Never once had Shackleton mentioned the presence during the long trek. Perhaps he was afraid his men might think he had lost his mind. But to his amazement, Worsley broke the silence.

"Boss," he said, "you know, I had a curious feeling on the march there was another person with us."

Quickly, Crean agreed. He had felt it too and been comforted and encouraged by it. But, like Shackleton, neither man had voiced his feelings aloud until that moment.

What could it have been that walked with Shackleton and his men during the hours they faced death in the lonely, tumbled wastes of a frozen island? Who was the Fourth Presence?

About the Author

Margaret Rau was born and grew up in China, the daughter of missionary parents. She attended college in the U.S. at Columbia, the University of Chicago, and the University of Redlands and is also a graduate of the Riverside College of Library Science. A freelance writer-photographer, she has written 16 books for children and several for adults, a movie in collaboration with the late Hollywood columnist (her husband) Neil Rau, and a six-part film strip about China. She speaks, reads, and writes Chinese and travels in China extensively. She has made several lengthy visits to Australia. She lives and works in Carpinteria, California.

About the Illustrator

Born in Vernon, Texas, Jim Sharpe attended Texas Tech before becoming a carrier jet pilot in the Navy. He later worked in Detroit as an art director, illustrator, and designer and in 1968 began his freelance career. His work includes many covers for *Time, TV Guide, Newsweek,* and others; illustrations for many magazines and books, and special commissions from government offices (including many postage stamps), the Olympics, Lincoln Center, the Kennedy Center, and PBS ("The Civil War"). His portrait of Gerald Ford is on display in the National Portrait Gallery's "Hall of Presidents." Jim now lives and works in Denton, Texas.

Index